D1401028

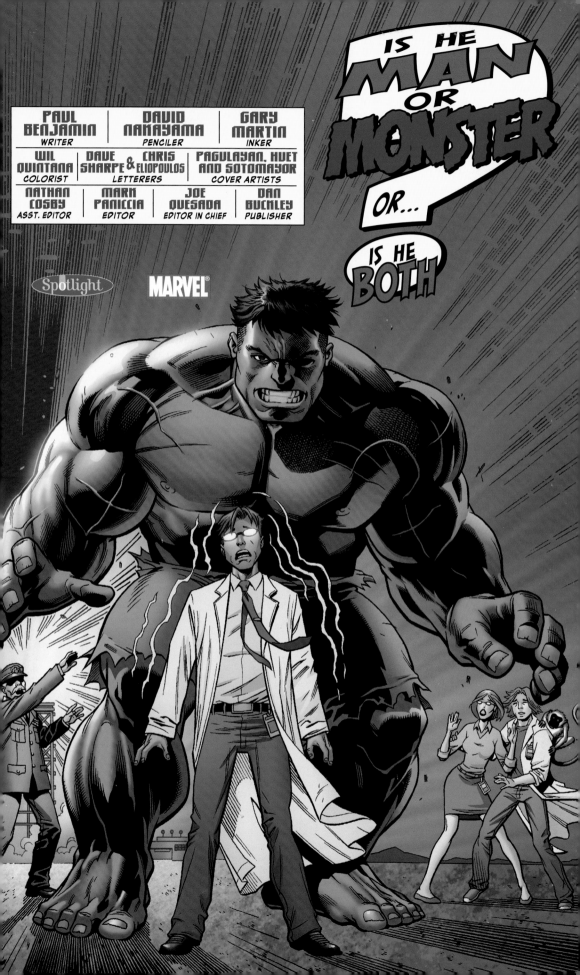

VISIT US AT
www.abdopublishing.com

Reinforced library bound edition published in 2009 by Spotlight, a division of the ABDO Publishing Group, 8000 West 78th Street, Edina, Minnesota 55439. Spotlight produces high-quality reinforced library bound editions for schools and libraries. Published by agreement with Marvel Characters, Inc.

Library of Congress Cataloging-in-Publication Data

Benjamin, Paul, 1970-
 Is he man or monster or--is he both? / Paul Benjamin, writer ; David Nakayama, penciler ; Gary Martin, inker ; Wil Quintana, colorist ; Dave Sharpe & Chris Eliooulos, letterers ; Pagulayan, Huet, and Sotomayor, cover artists. -- Reinforced library bound ed.
     p. cm. -- (Hulk)
 "Marvel."
 Summary: "Caught in a blast of gamma radiation, brilliant scientist Bruce Banner now finds himself in times of stress turning into the living engine of destruction know as THE INCREDIBLE HULK!"-- Provided by publisher.
 ISBN 978-1-59961-547-9
 1. Graphic novels. [1. Graphic novels.] I. Nakayama, David, ill. II. Title.
 PZ7.7.B45Is 2008
 [Fic]--dc22
                                                                          2007052759

All Spotlight books have reinforced library bindings and are manufactured in the United States of America.

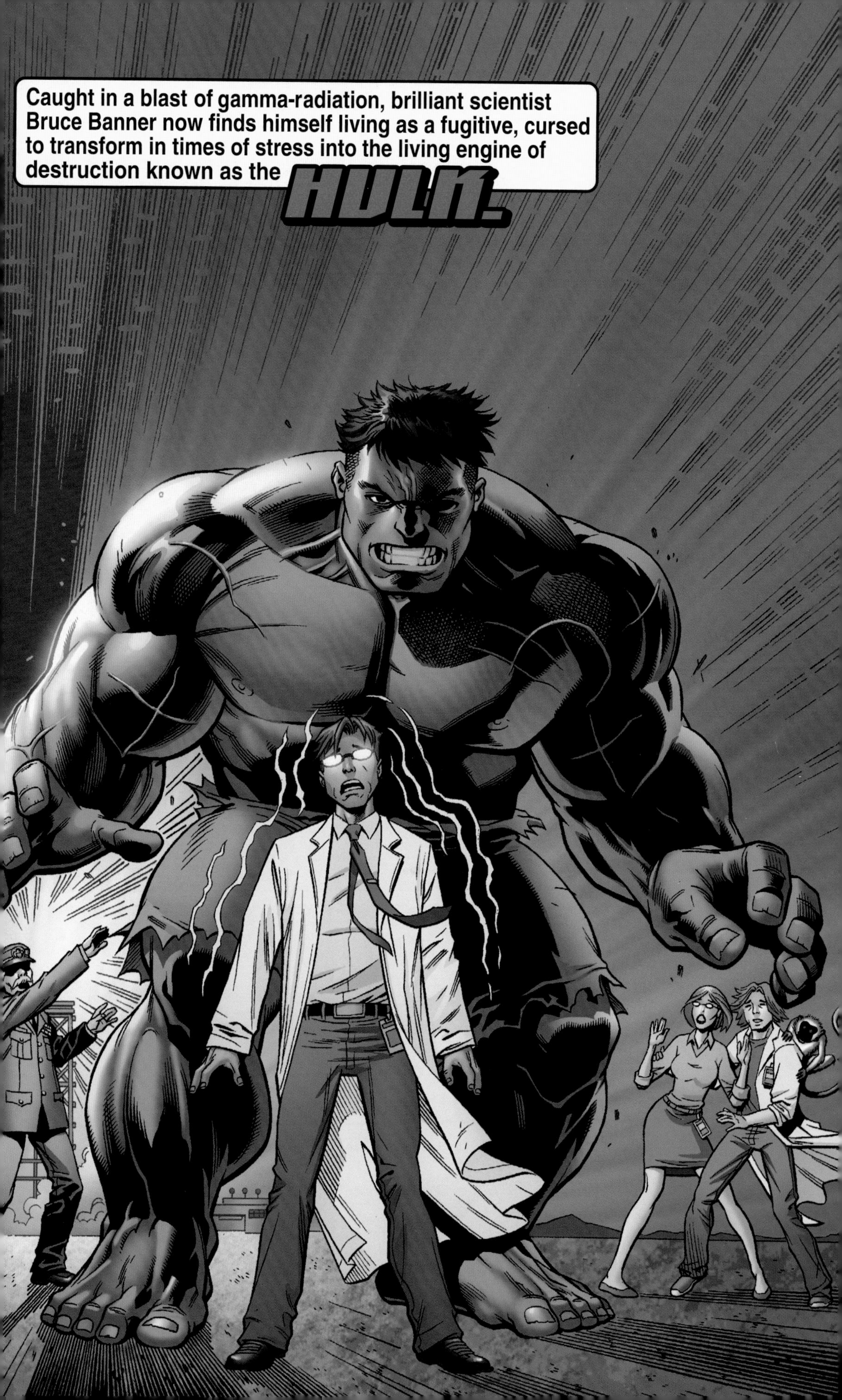
Caught in a blast of gamma-radiation, brilliant scientist Bruce Banner now finds himself living as a fugitive, cursed to transform in times of stress into the living engine of destruction known as the
HULK.

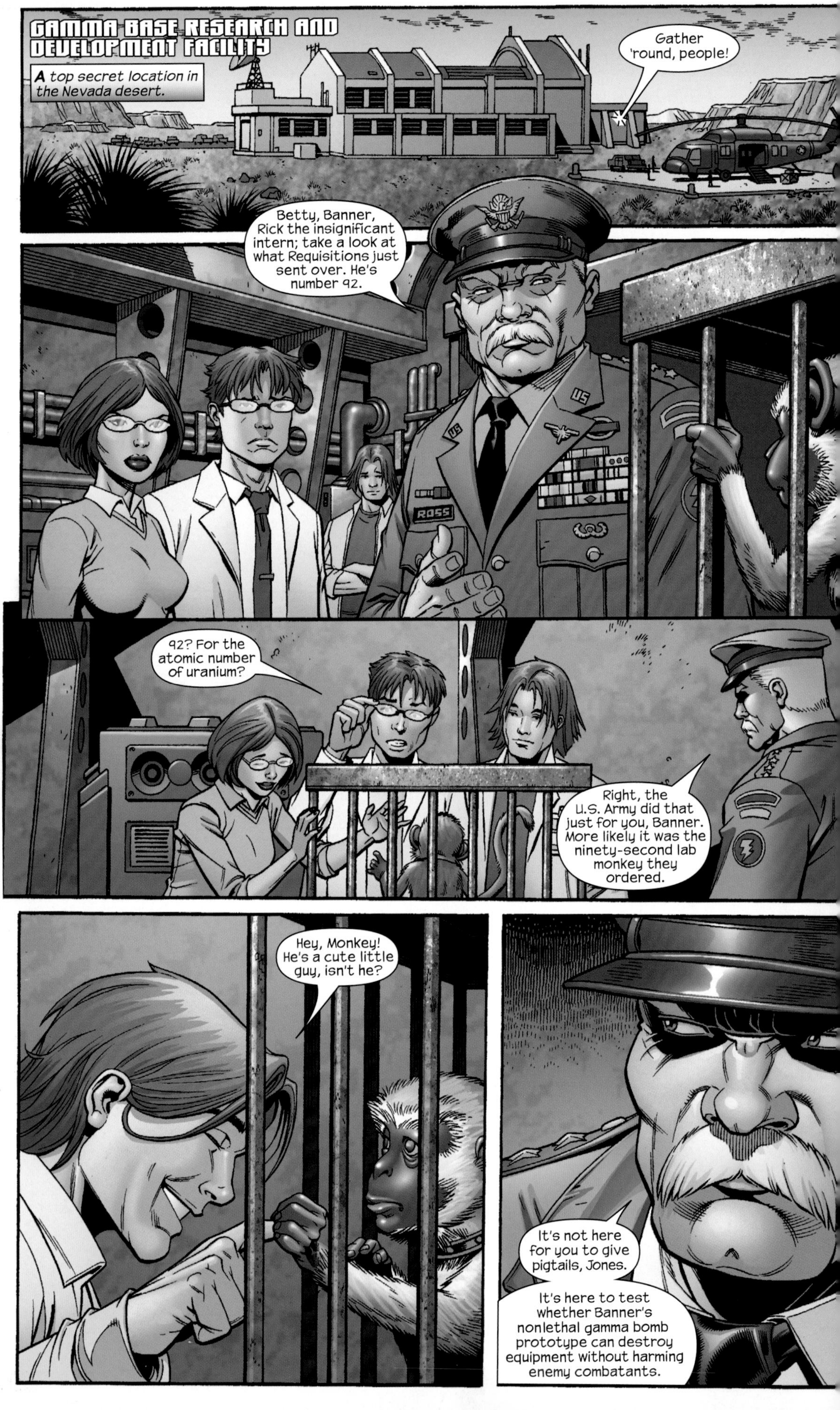
GAMMA BASE RESEARCH AND DEVELOPMENT FACILITY
A top secret location in the Nevada desert.
Gather 'round, people!
Betty, Banner, Rick the insignificant intern; take a look at what Requisitions just sent over. He's number 92.
ROSS
92? For the atomic number of uranium?
Right, the U.S. Army did that just for you, Banner. More likely it was the ninety-second lab monkey they ordered.
Hey, Monkey! He's a cute little guy, isn't he?
It's not here for you to give pigtails, Jones.
It's here to test whether Banner's nonlethal gamma bomb prototype can destroy equipment without harming enemy combatants.

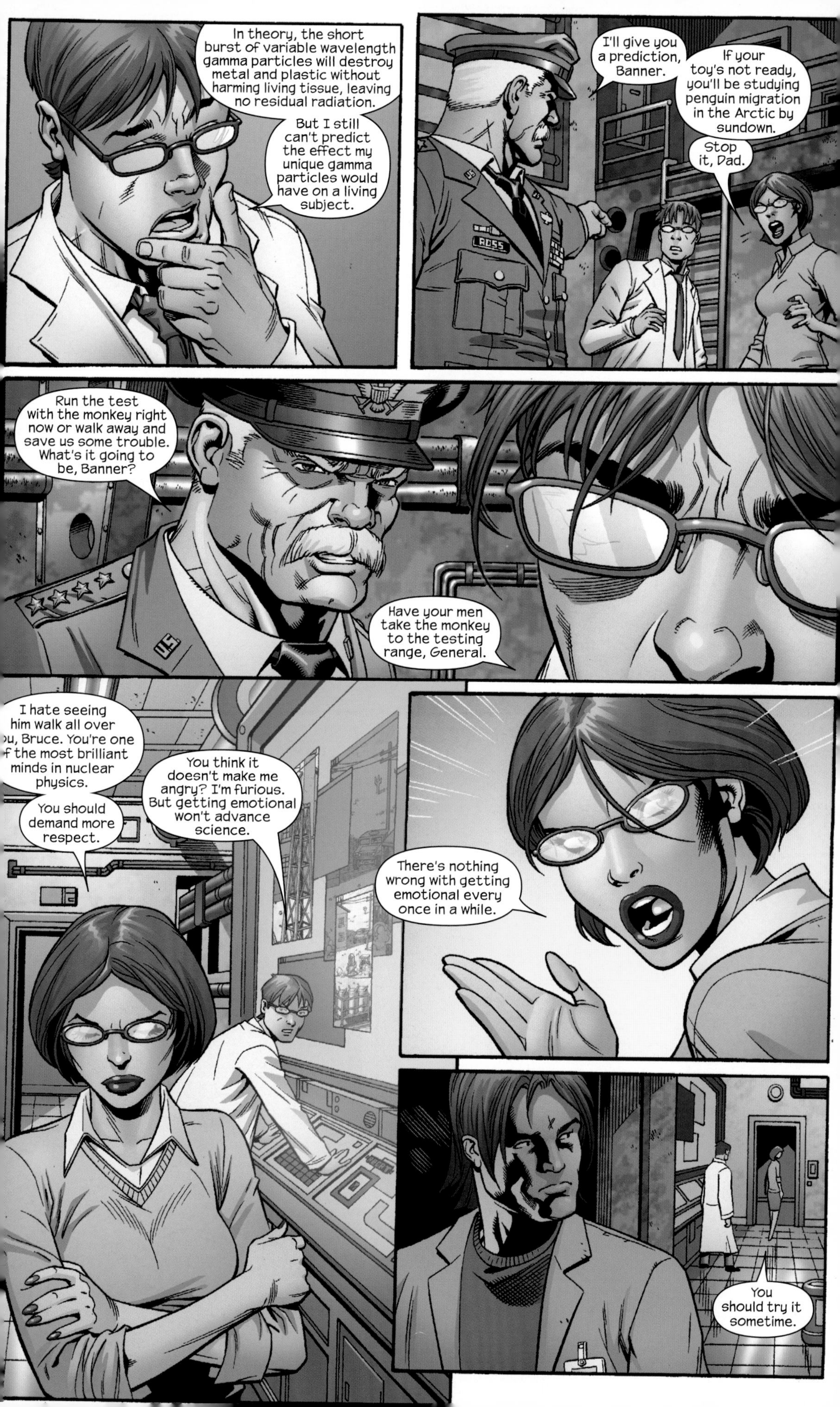
In theory, the short burst of variable wavelength gamma particles will destroy metal and plastic without harming living tissue, leaving no residual radiation.
But I still can't predict the effect my unique gamma particles would have on a living subject.
I'll give you a prediction, Banner.
If your toy's not ready, you'll be studying penguin migration in the Arctic by sundown.
Stop it, Dad.
ROSS
Run the test with the monkey right now or walk away and save us some trouble. What's it going to be, Banner?
Have your men take the monkey to the testing range, General.
I hate seeing him walk all over you, Bruce. You're one of the most brilliant minds in nuclear physics.
You should demand more respect.
You think it doesn't make me angry? I'm furious. But getting emotional won't advance science.
There's nothing wrong with getting emotional every once in a while.
You should try it sometime.

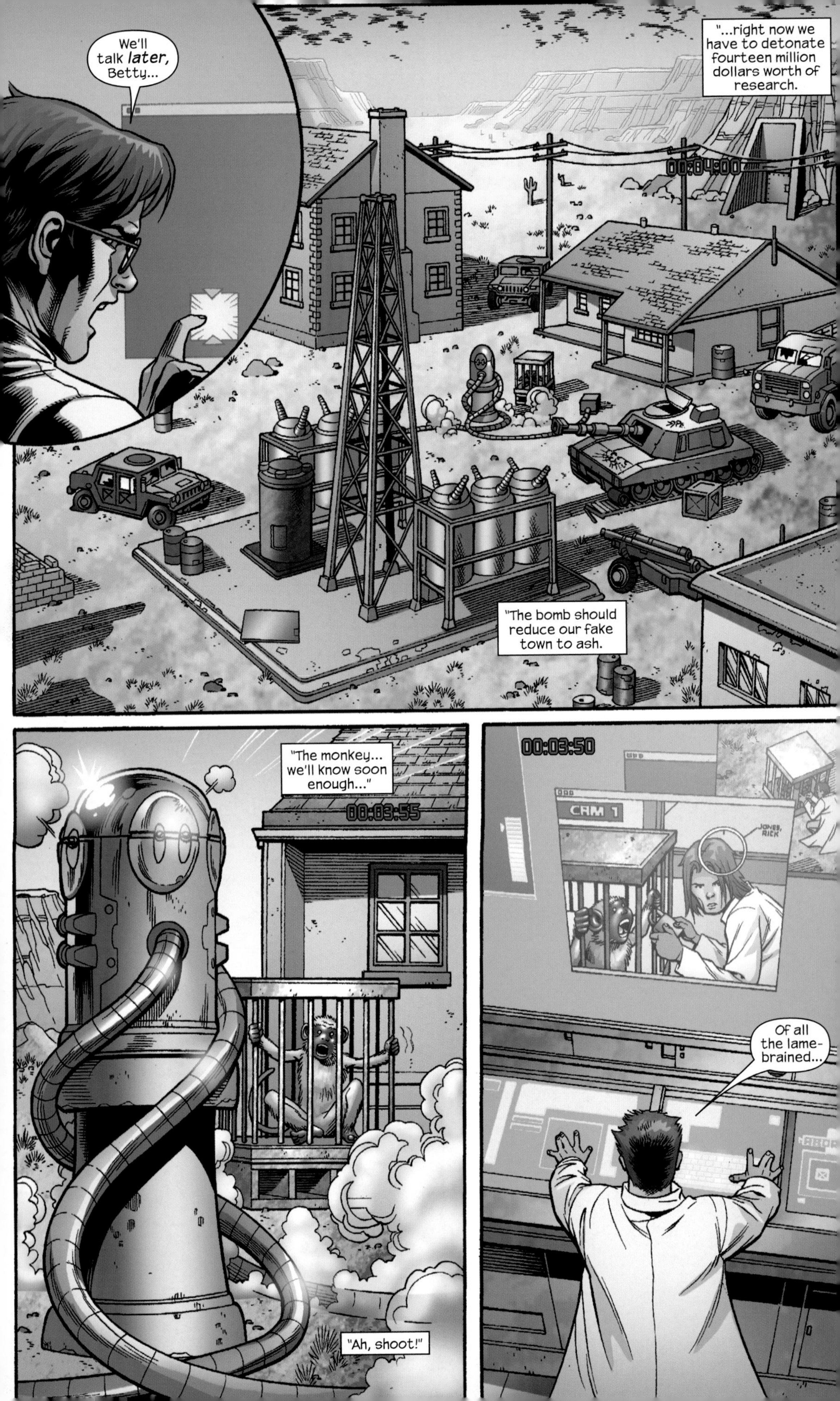
We'll talk *later,* Betty...
"...right now we have to detonate fourteen million dollars worth of research.
00:04:00
"The bomb should reduce our fake town to ash.
"The monkey... we'll know soon enough..."
00:03:55
"Ah, shoot!"
00:03:50
CAM 1
JONES, RICK
Of all the lame-brained...

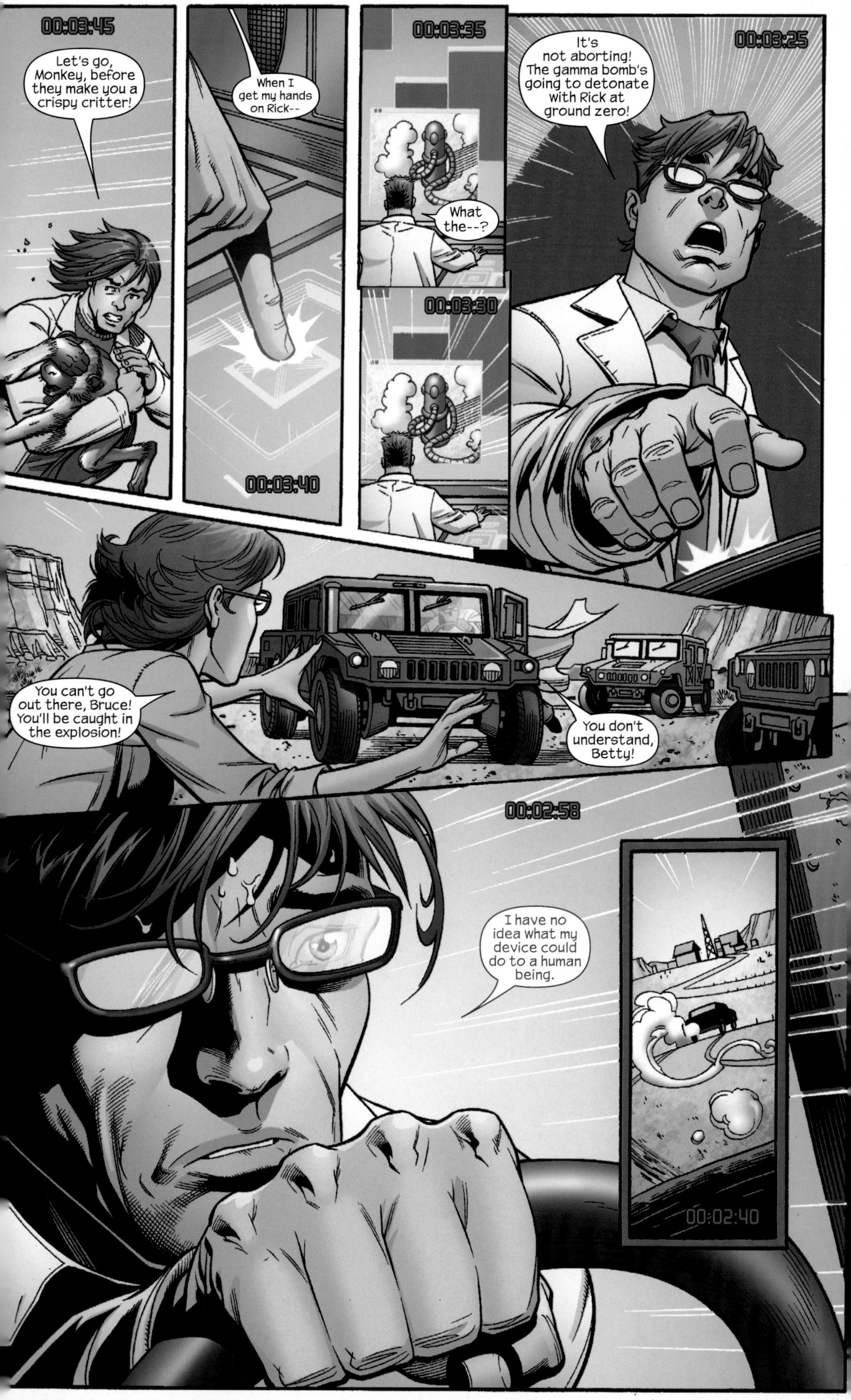
00:03:45
Let's go, Monkey, before they make you a crispy critter!
When I get my hands on Rick--
00:03:40
00:03:35
What the--?
00:03:30
It's not aborting! The gamma bomb's going to detonate with Rick at ground zero!
00:03:25
You can't go out there, Bruce! You'll be caught in the explosion!
You don't understand, Betty!
00:02:58
I have no idea what my device could do to a human being.
00:02:40

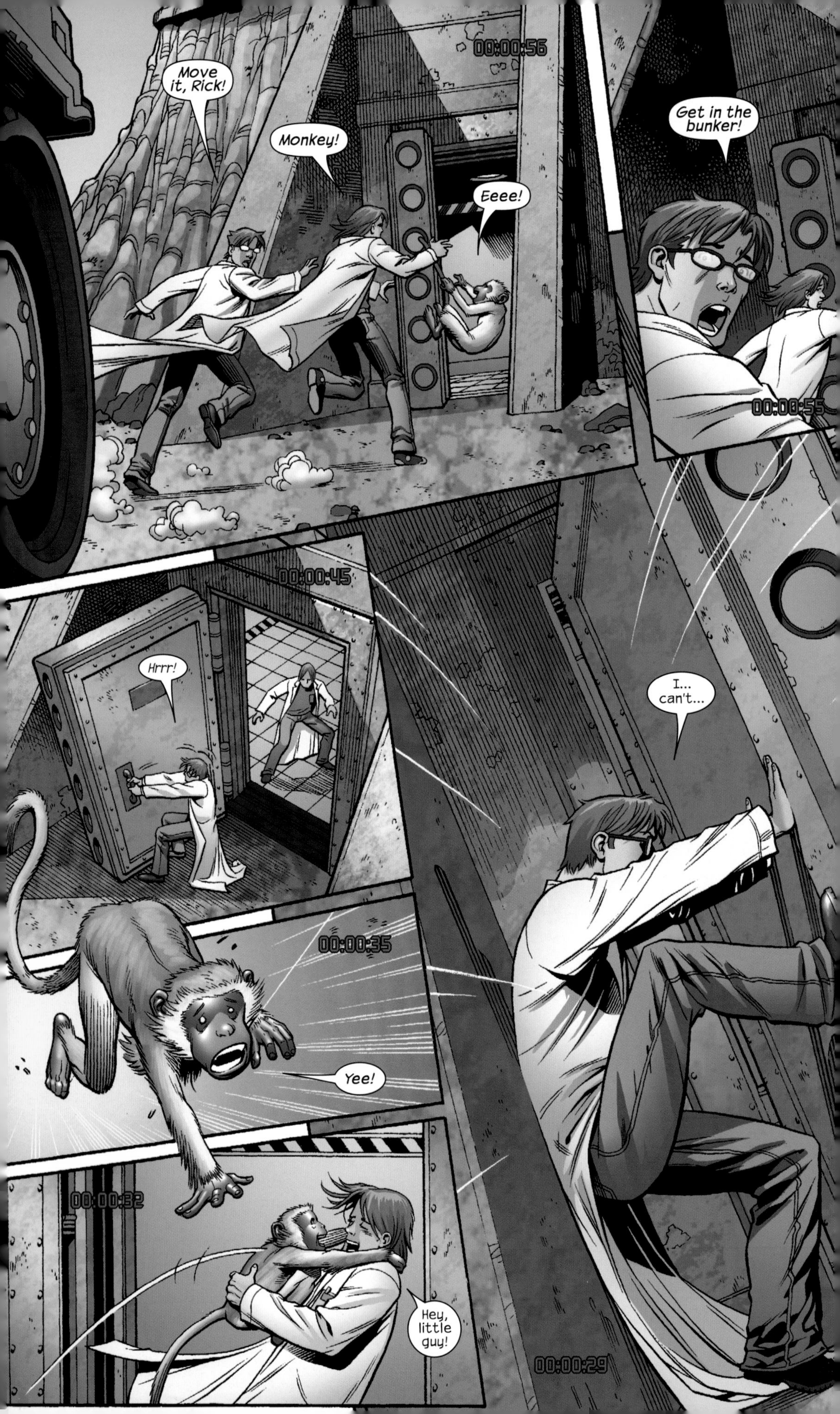
00:00:56
Move it, Rick!
Monkey!
Eeee!
Get in the bunker!
00:00:55
00:00:45
Hrrr!
I... can't...
00:00:35
Yee!
00:00:32
Hey, little guy!
00:00:29

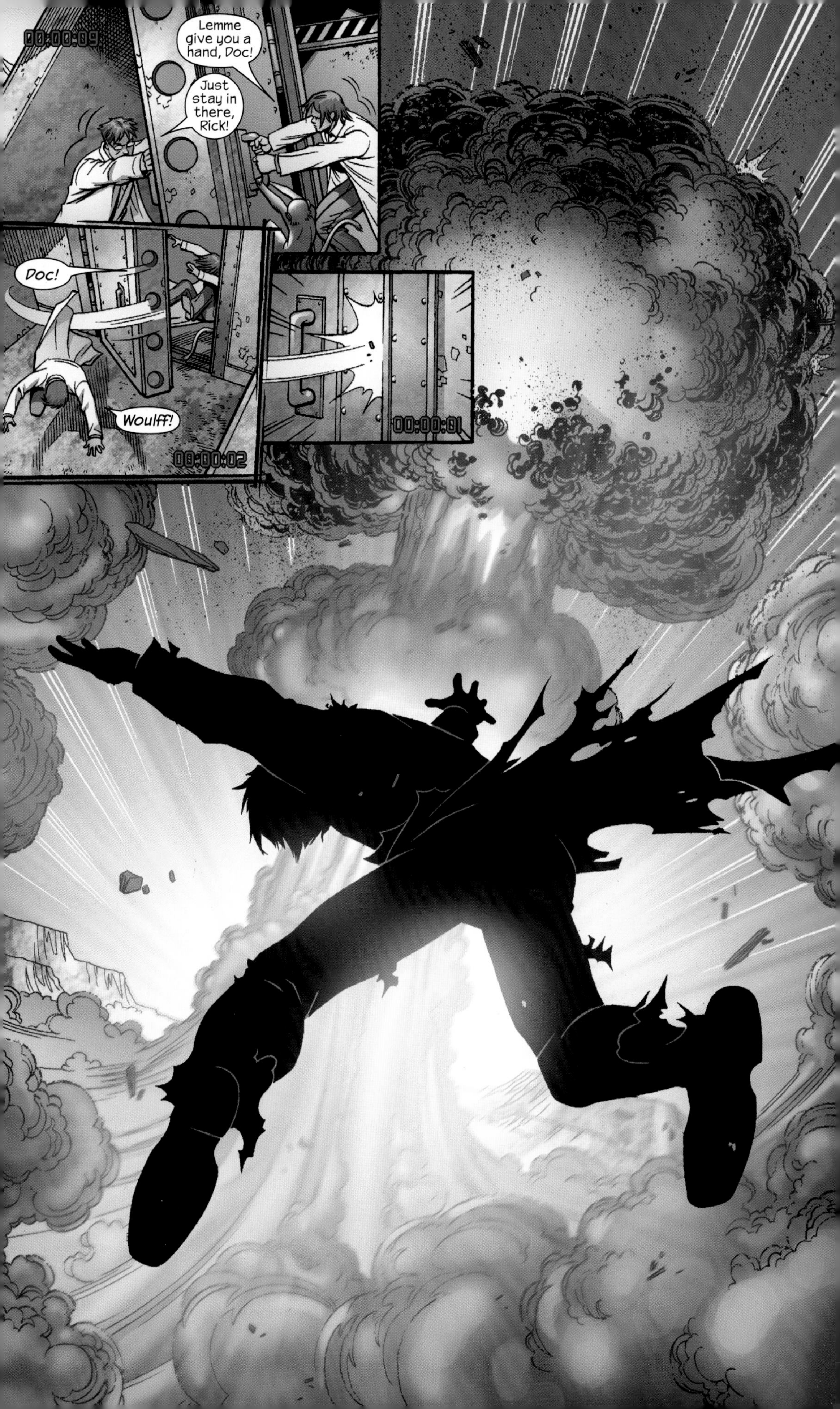
00:00:09
Lemme give you a hand, Doc!
Just stay in there, Rick!
Doc!
Woulff!
00:00:02
00:00:01

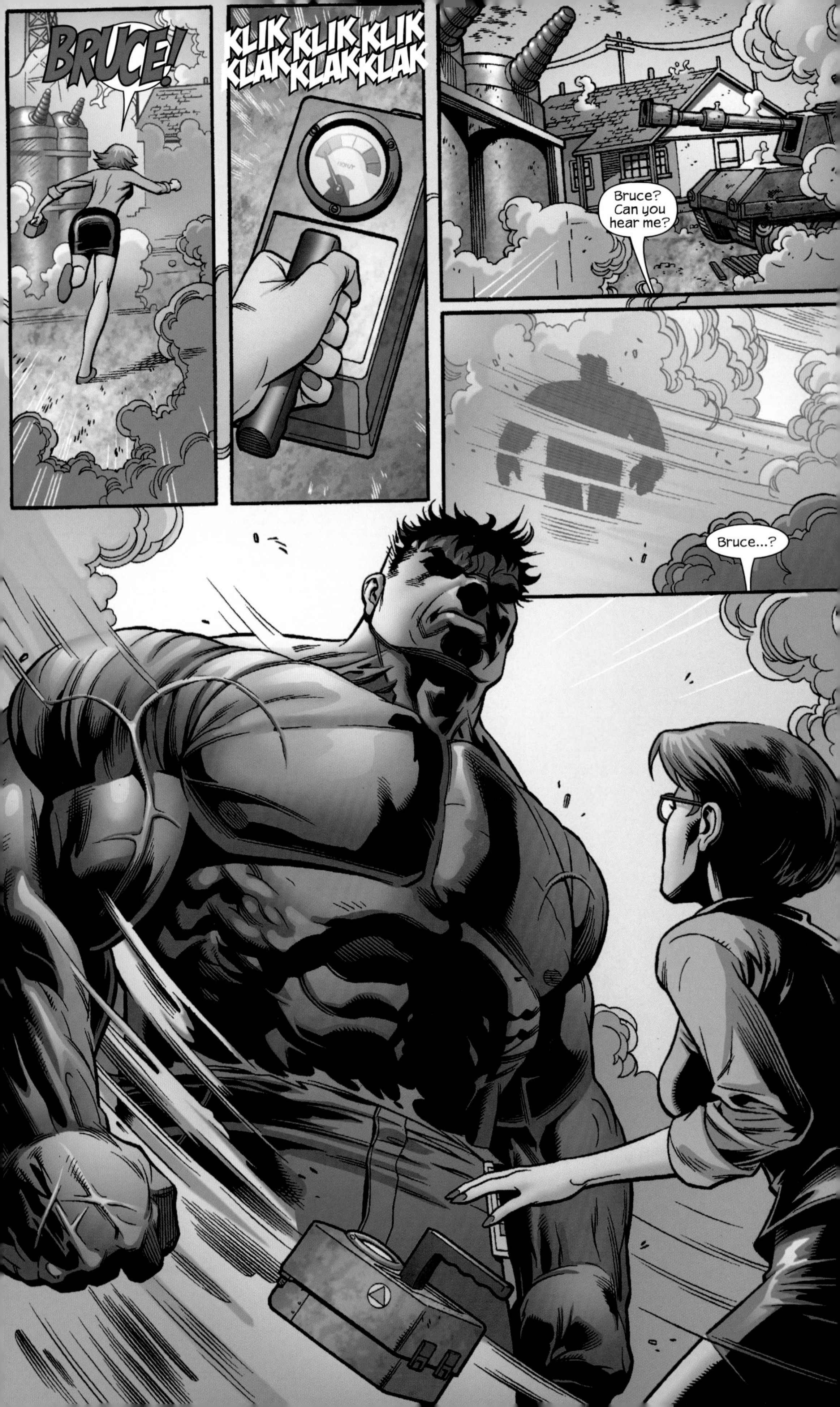
BRUCE!
KLIK KLAK KLIK KLAK KLIK KLAK
Bruce? Can you hear me?
Bruce...?

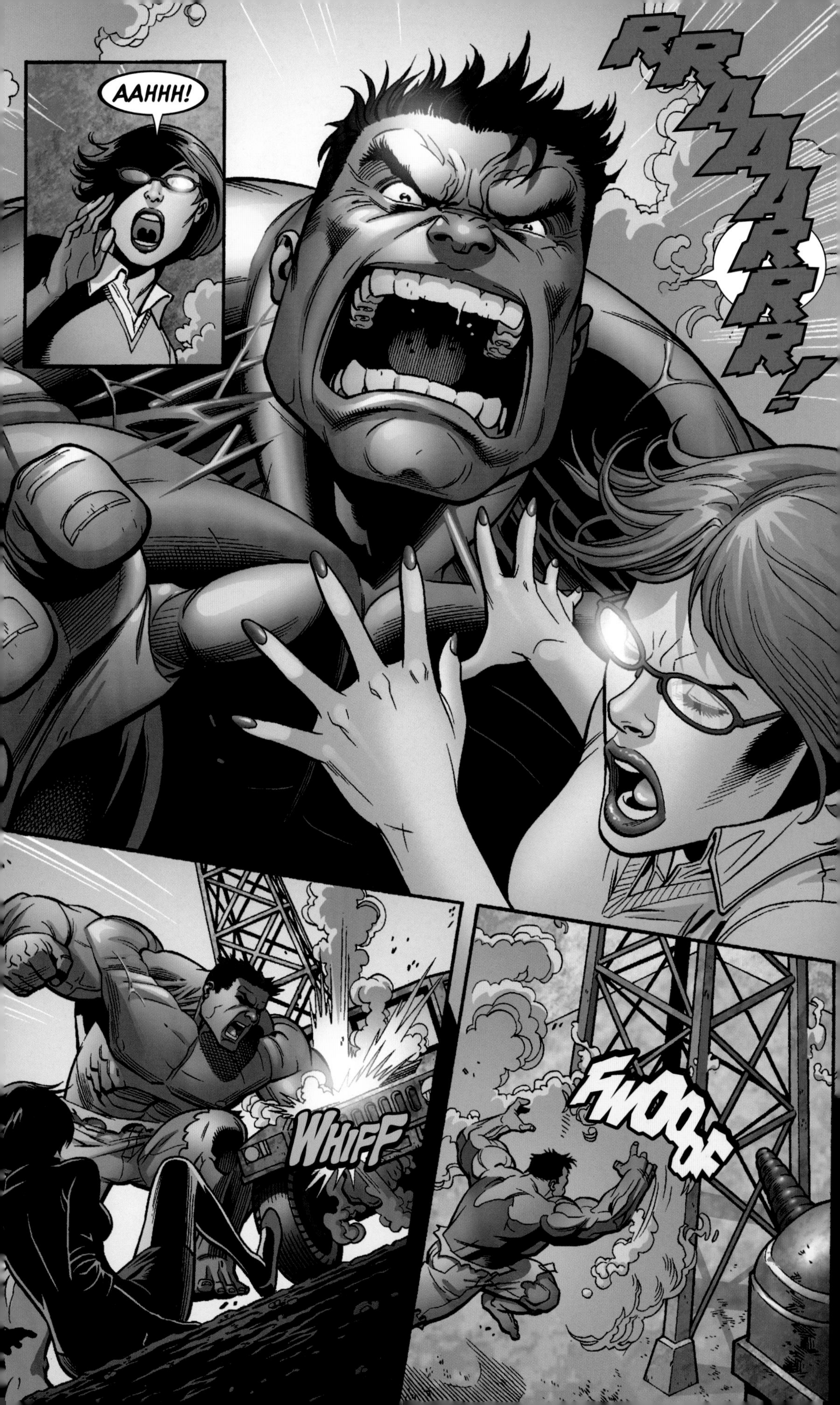

AAHHH!
RRAAARRR!
WHIFF
FWOOF

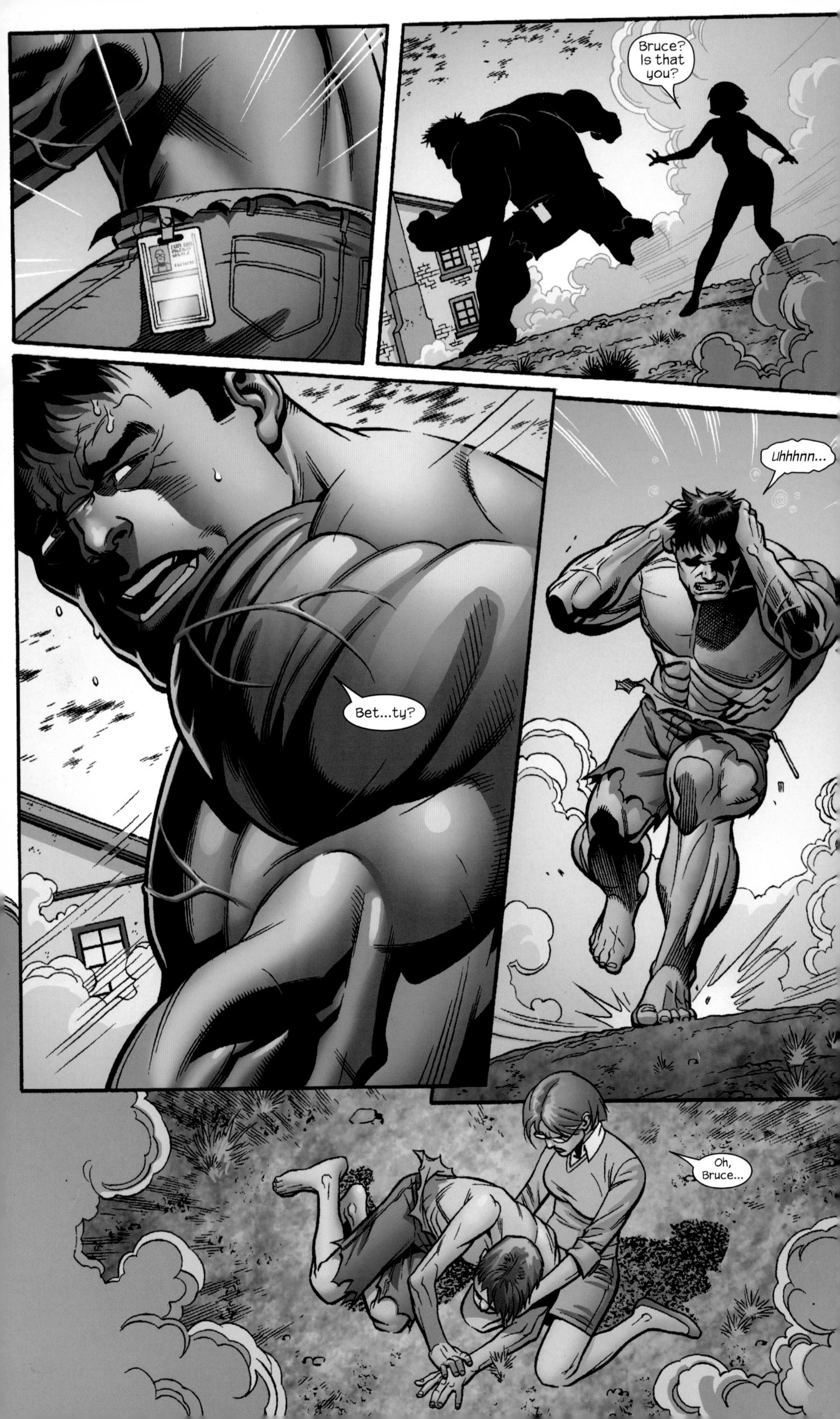
Bruce? Is that you?
Bet...ty?
Uhhhnn...
Oh, Bruce...

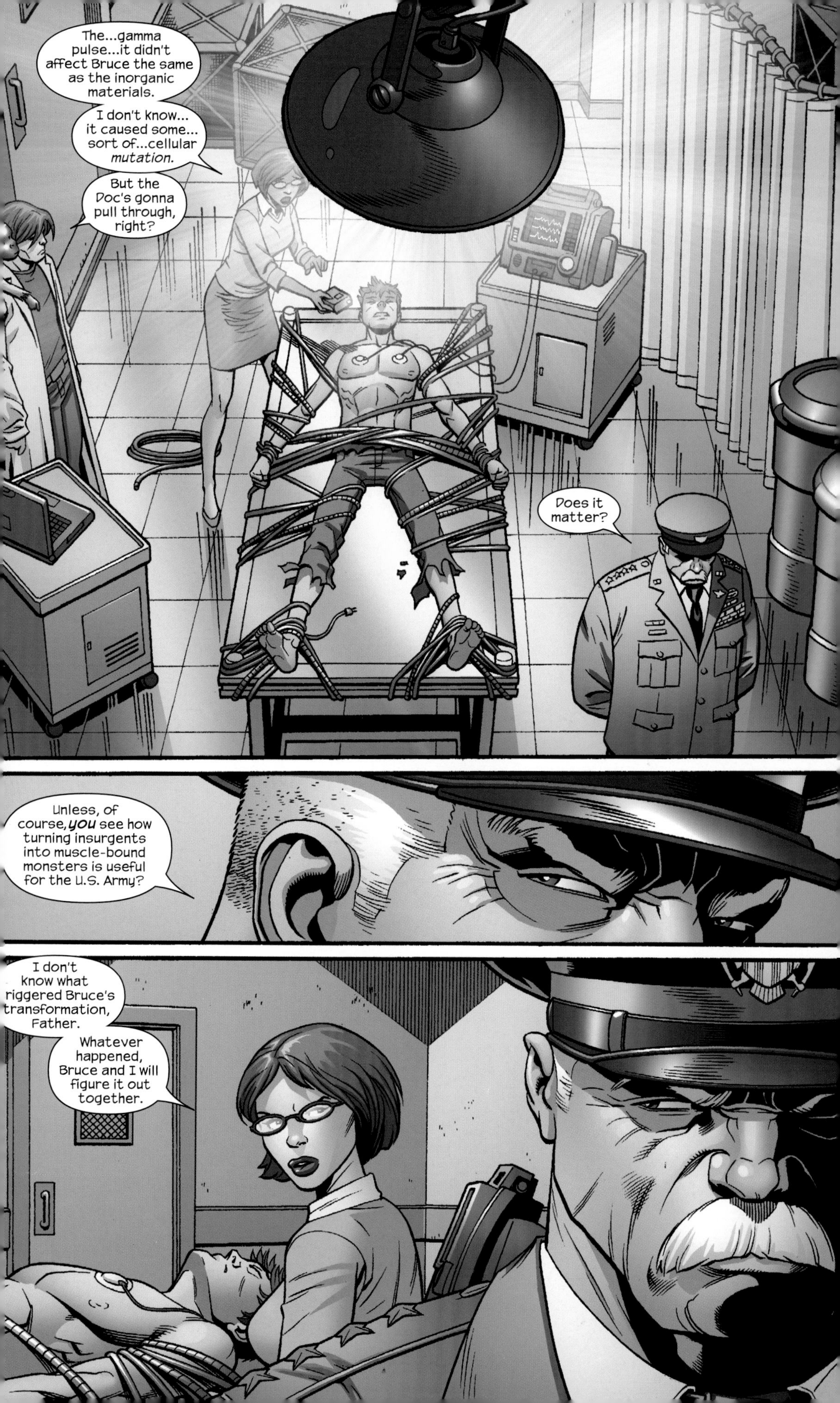
The...gamma pulse...it didn't affect Bruce the same as the inorganic materials.
I don't know... it caused some... sort of...cellular *mutation.*
But the Doc's gonna pull through, right?
Does it matter?
Unless, of course, ***you*** see how turning insurgents into muscle-bound monsters is useful for the U.S. Army?
I don't know what riggered Bruce's transformation, Father.
Whatever happened, Bruce and I will figure it out together.

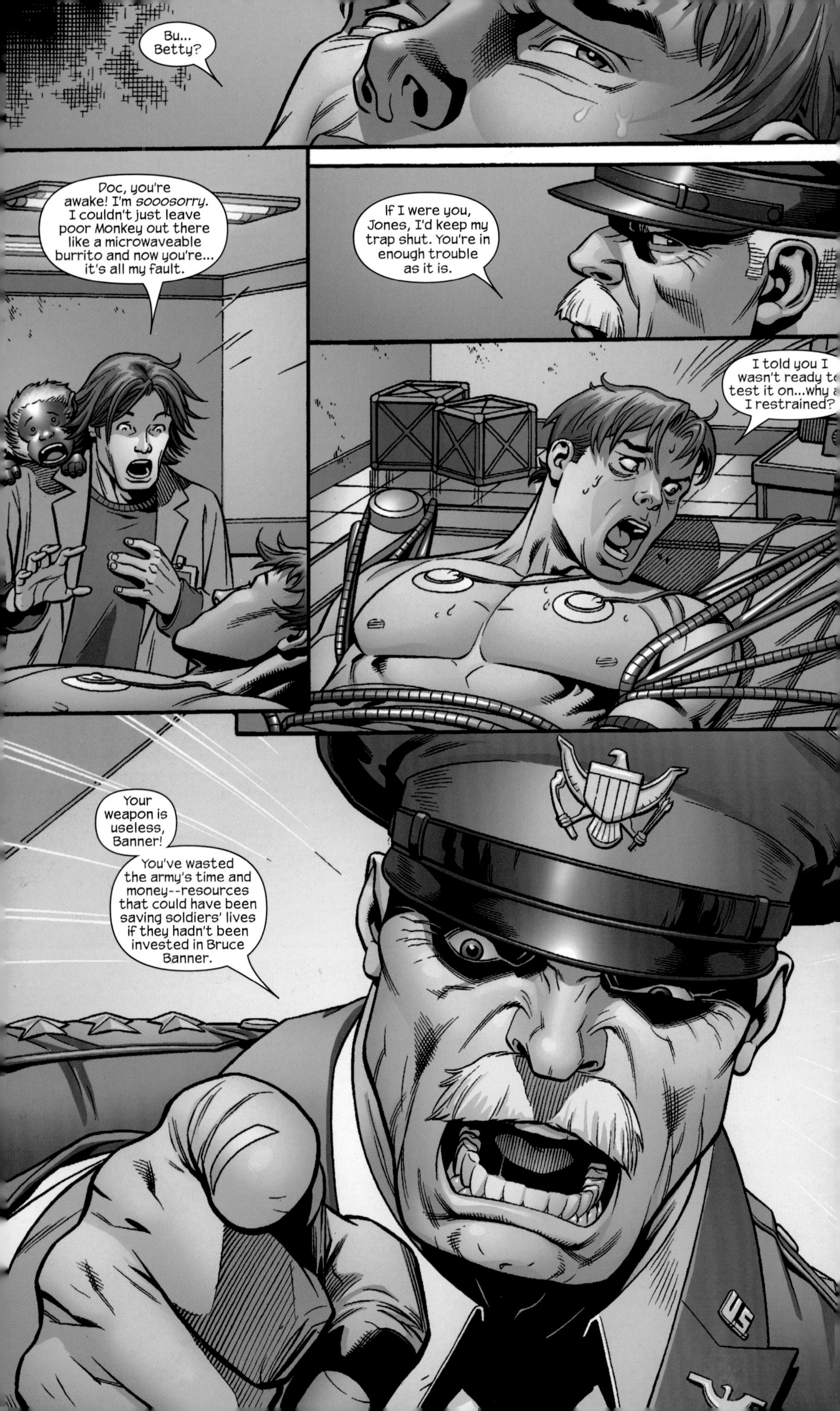
Bu... Betty?
Doc, you're awake! I'm *sooosorry.* I couldn't just leave poor Monkey out there like a microwaveable burrito and now you're... it's all my fault.
If I were you, Jones, I'd keep my trap shut. You're in enough trouble as it is.
I told you I wasn't ready to test it on...why a I restrained?
Your weapon is useless, Banner!
You've wasted the army's time and money--resources that could have been saving soldiers' lives if they hadn't been invested in Bruce Banner.

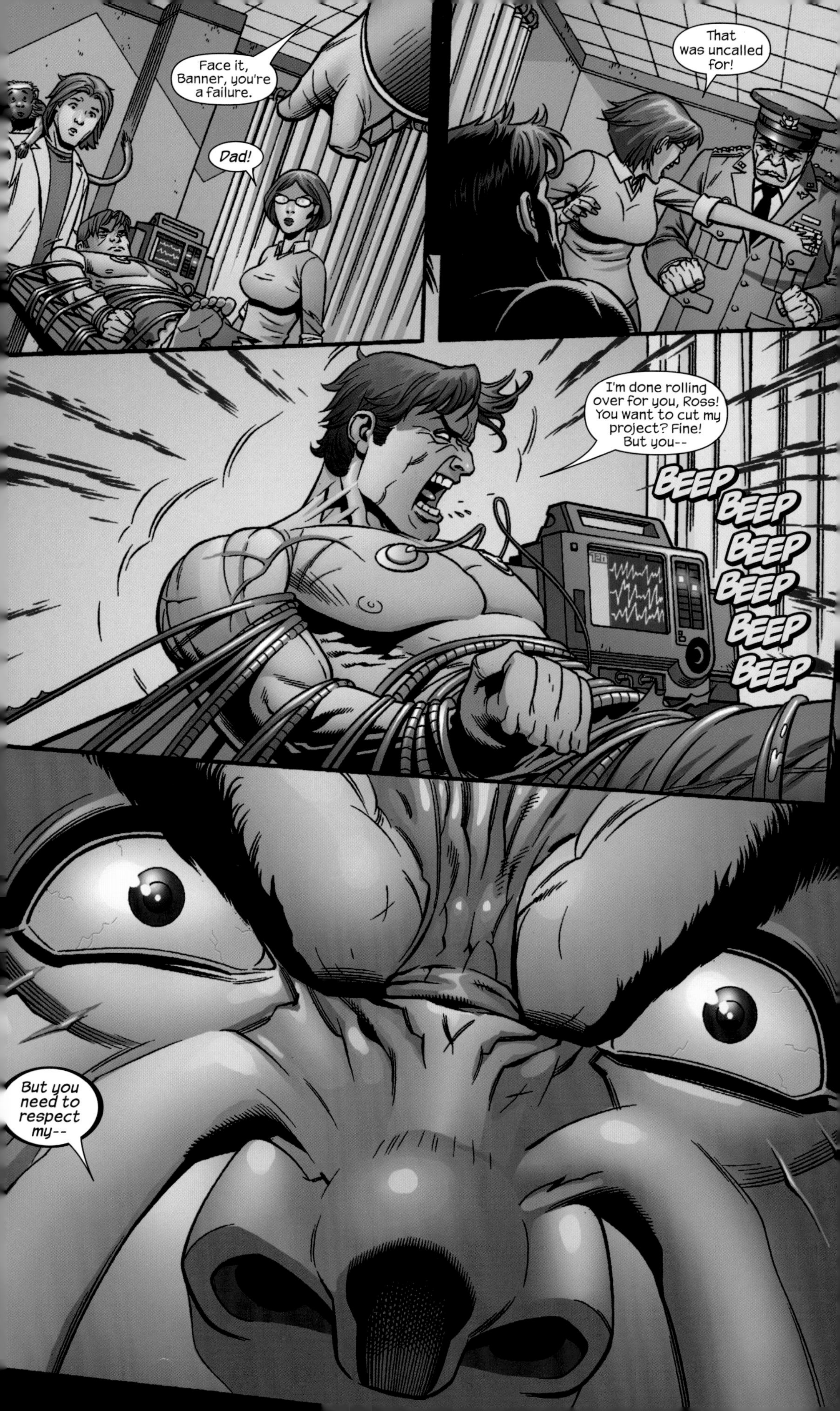
Face it, Banner, you're a failure.
Dad!
That was uncalled for!
I'm done rolling over for you, Ross! You want to cut my project? Fine! But you--
BEEP BEEP BEEP BEEP BEEP BEEP
But you need to respect my--

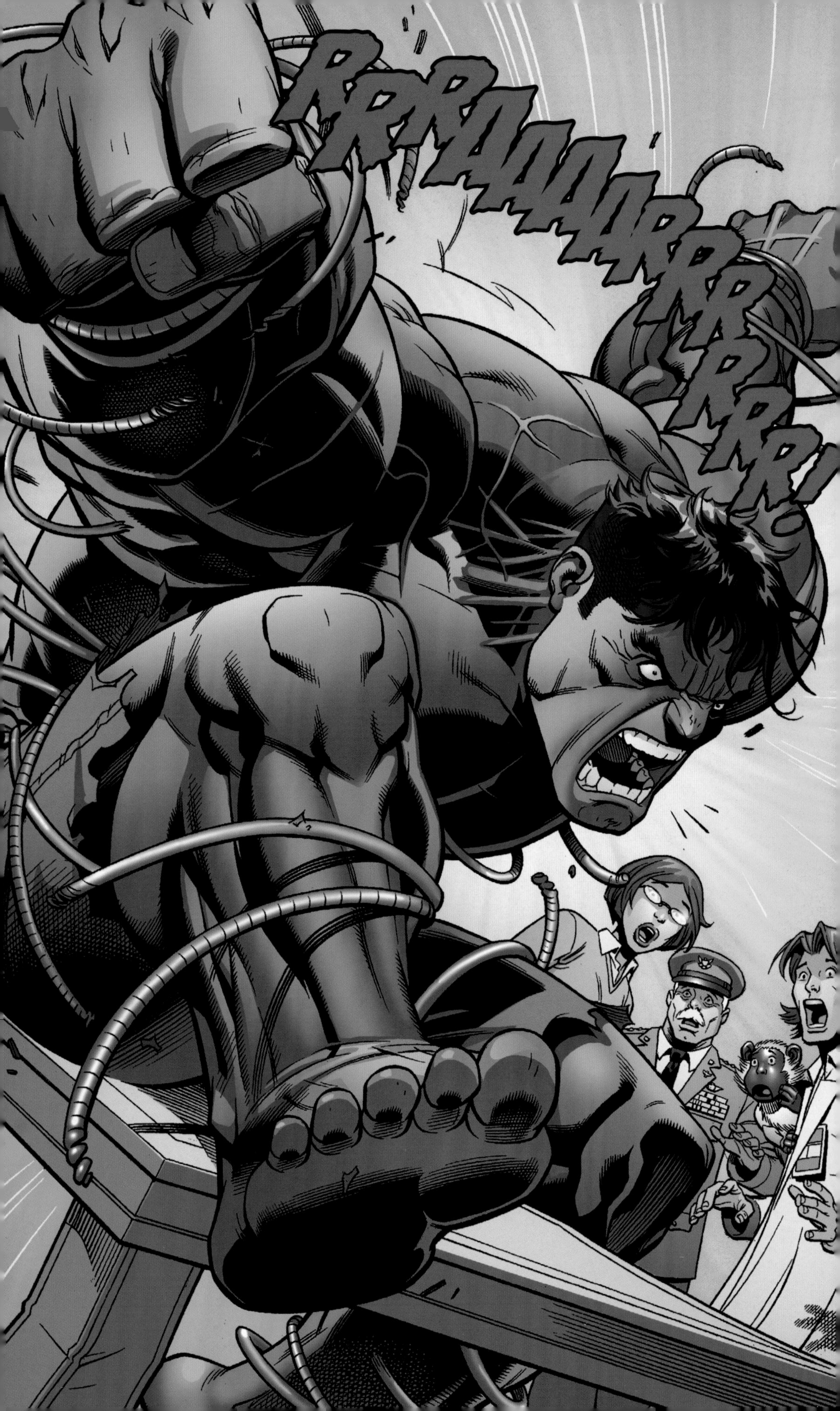

RRRAAAARRRRRR!

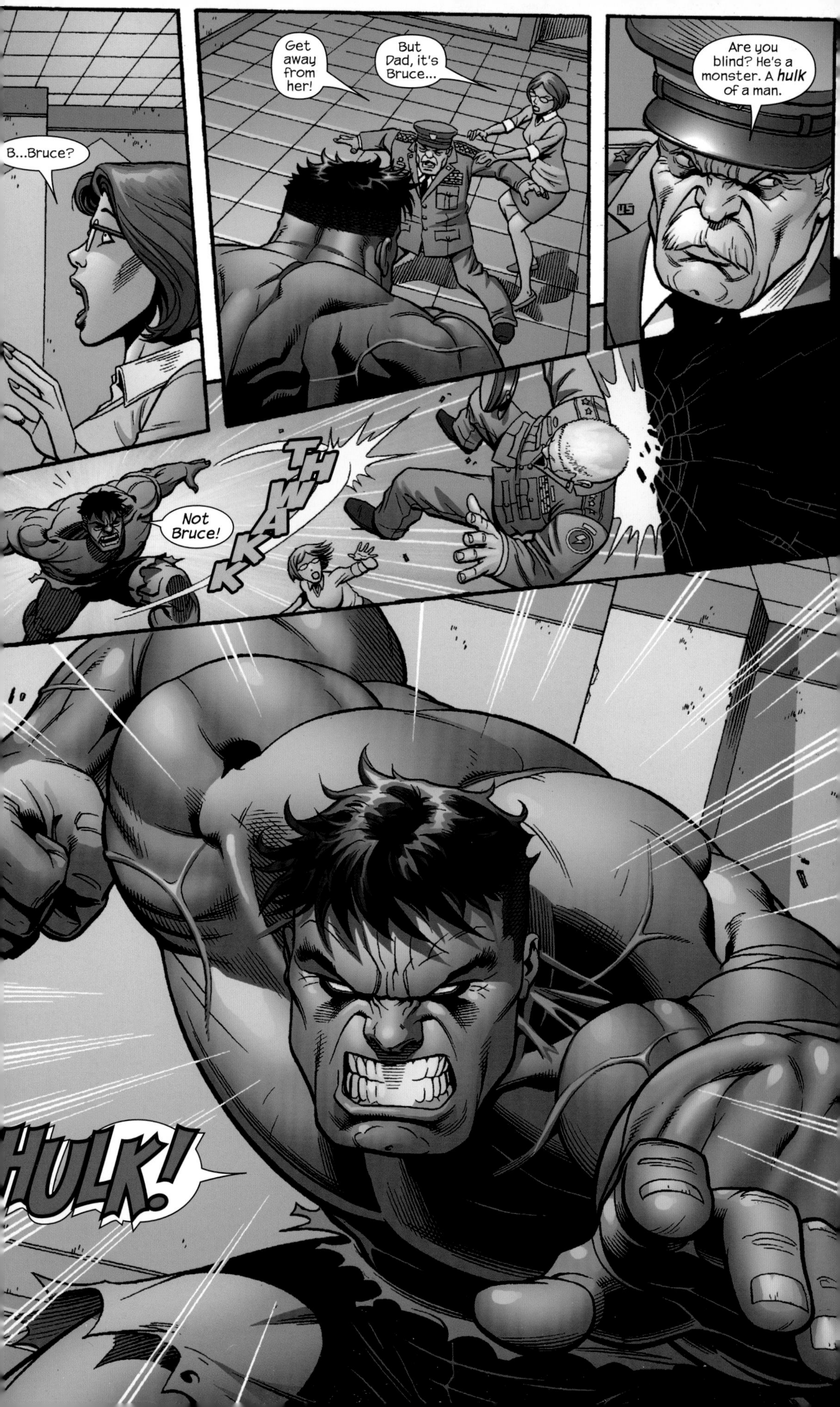
B...Bruce?
Get away from her!
But Dad, it's Bruce...
Are you blind? He's a monster. A *hulk* of a man.
Not Bruce!
THWAKKK
HULK!

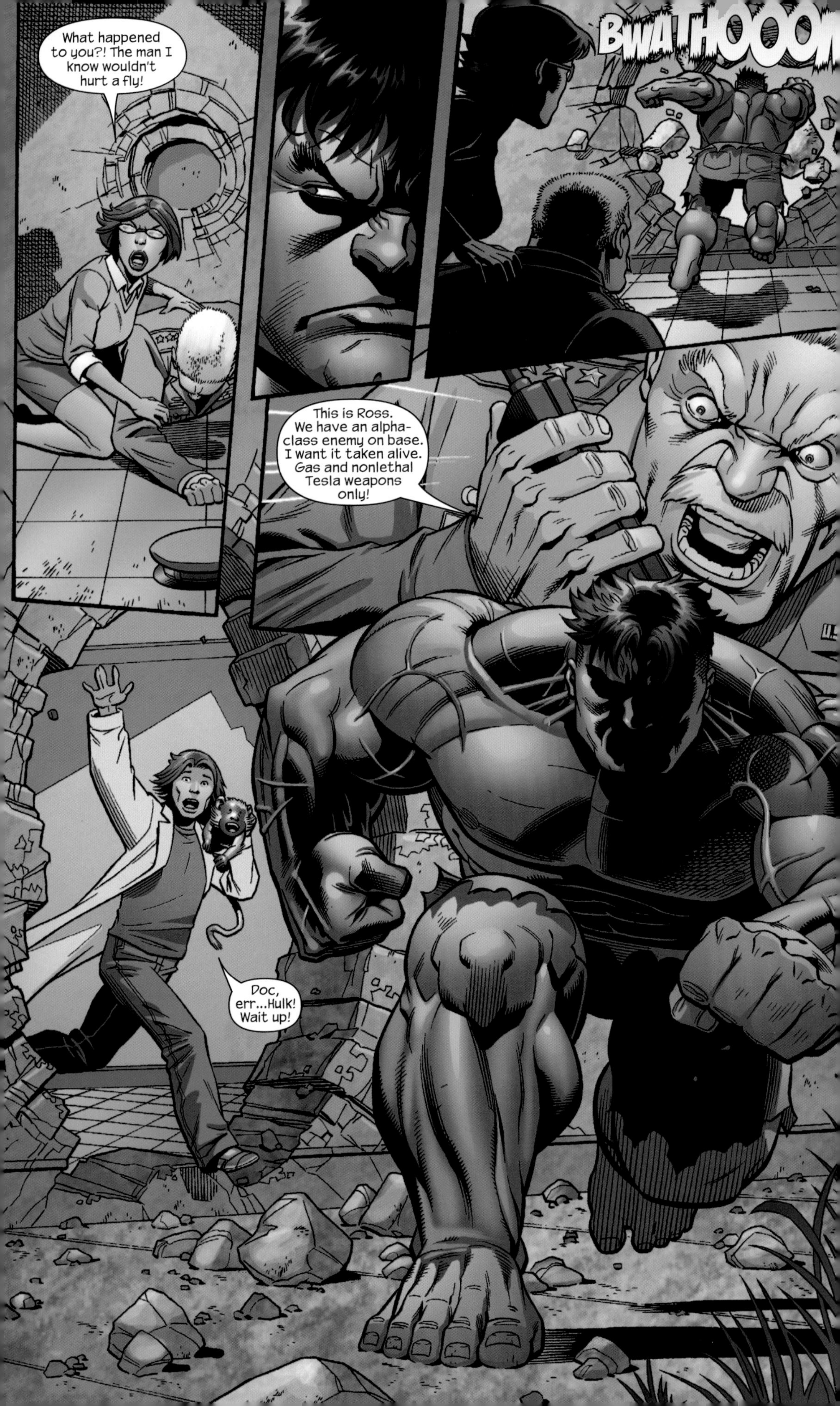
What happened to you?! The man I know wouldn't hurt a fly!
BWATHOOOM
This is Ross. We have an alpha-class enemy on base. I want it taken alive. Gas and nonlethal Tesla weapons only!
Doc, err...Hulk! Wait up!

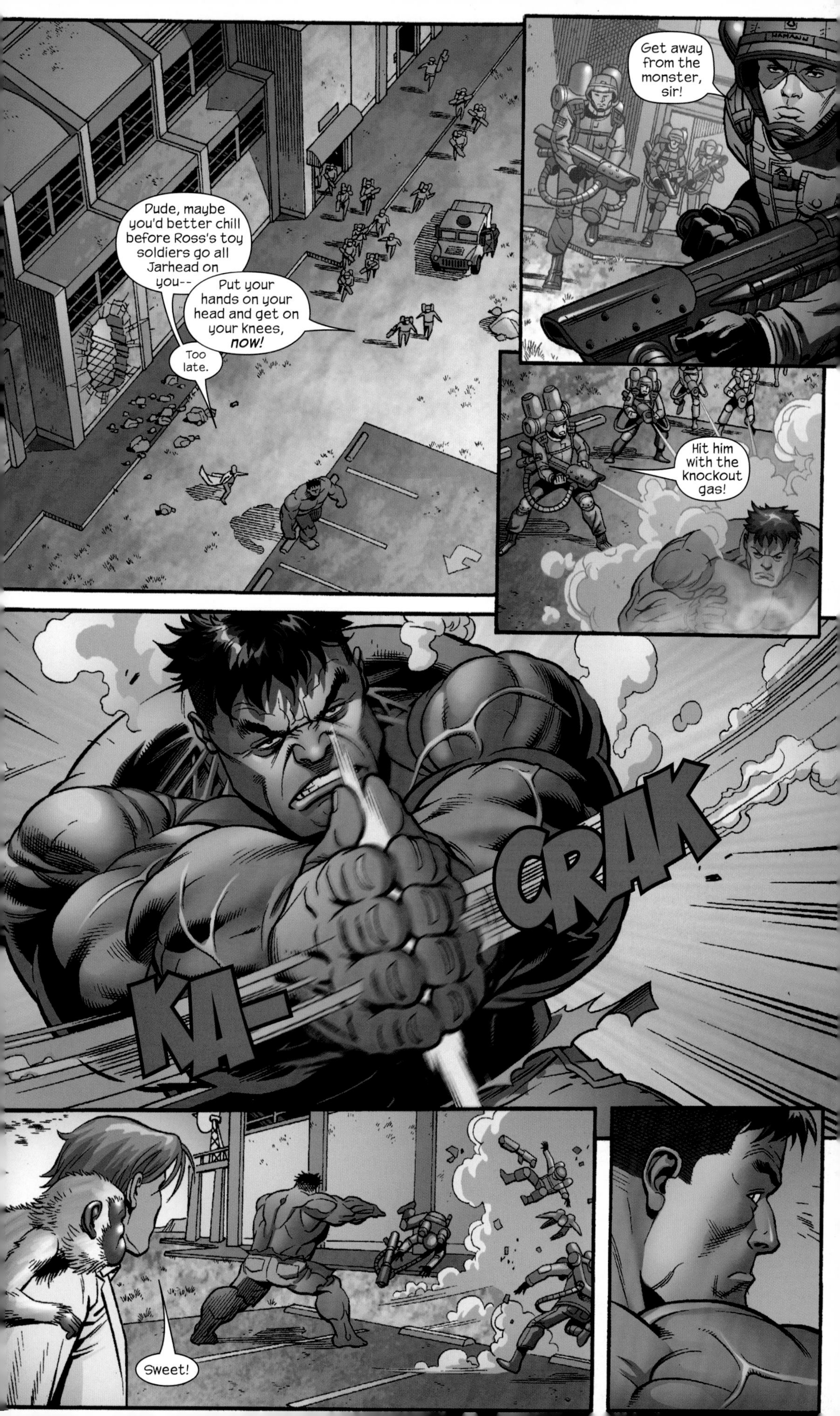
Dude, maybe you'd better chill before Ross's toy soldiers go all Jarhead on you--
Put your hands on your head and get on your knees, NOW!
Too late.
Get away from the monster, sir!
Hit him with the knockout gas!
KA-
CRAK
Sweet!

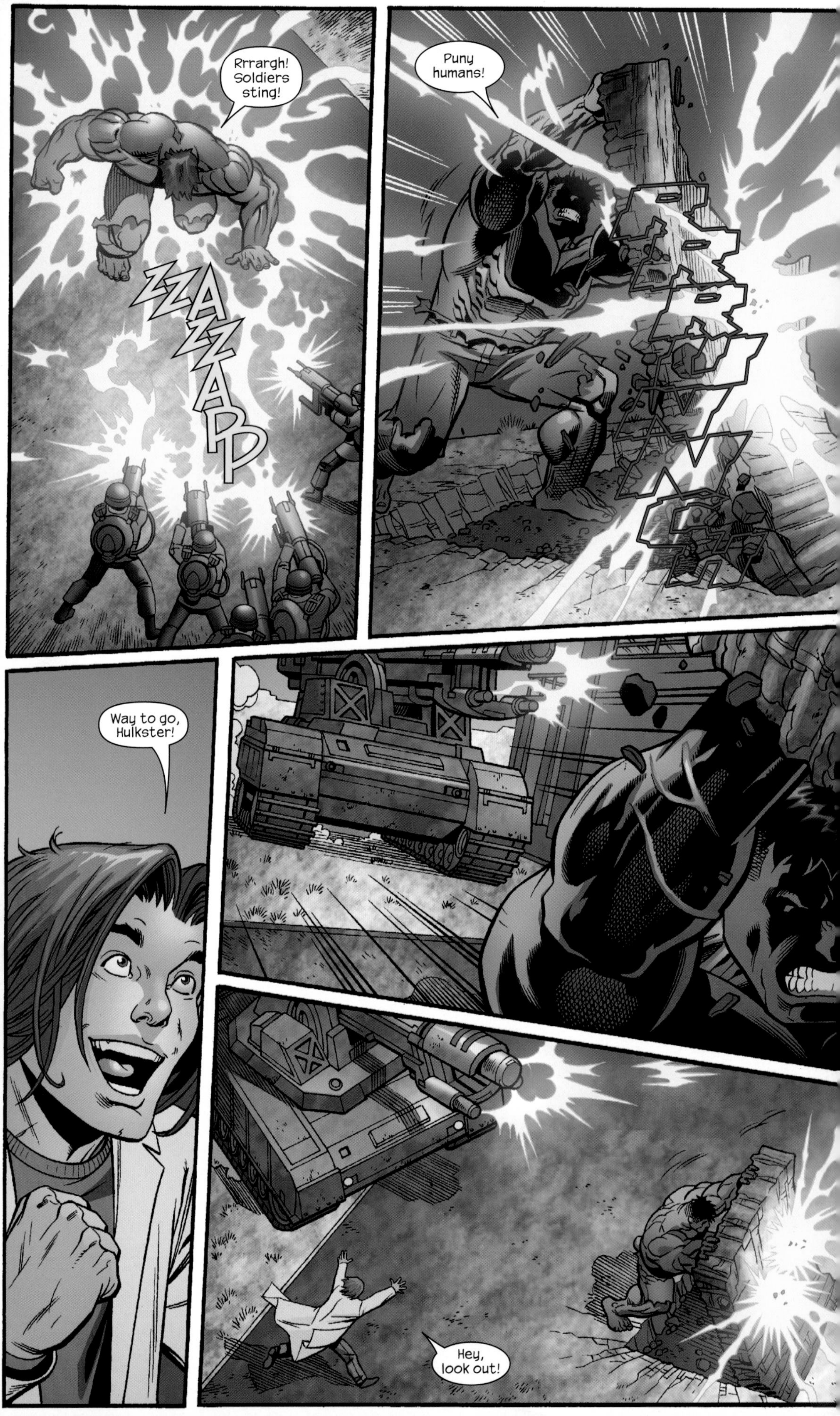
Rrrargh! Soldiers sting!
ZZZAZZAPP
Puny humans!
Way to go, Hulkster!
Hey, look out!

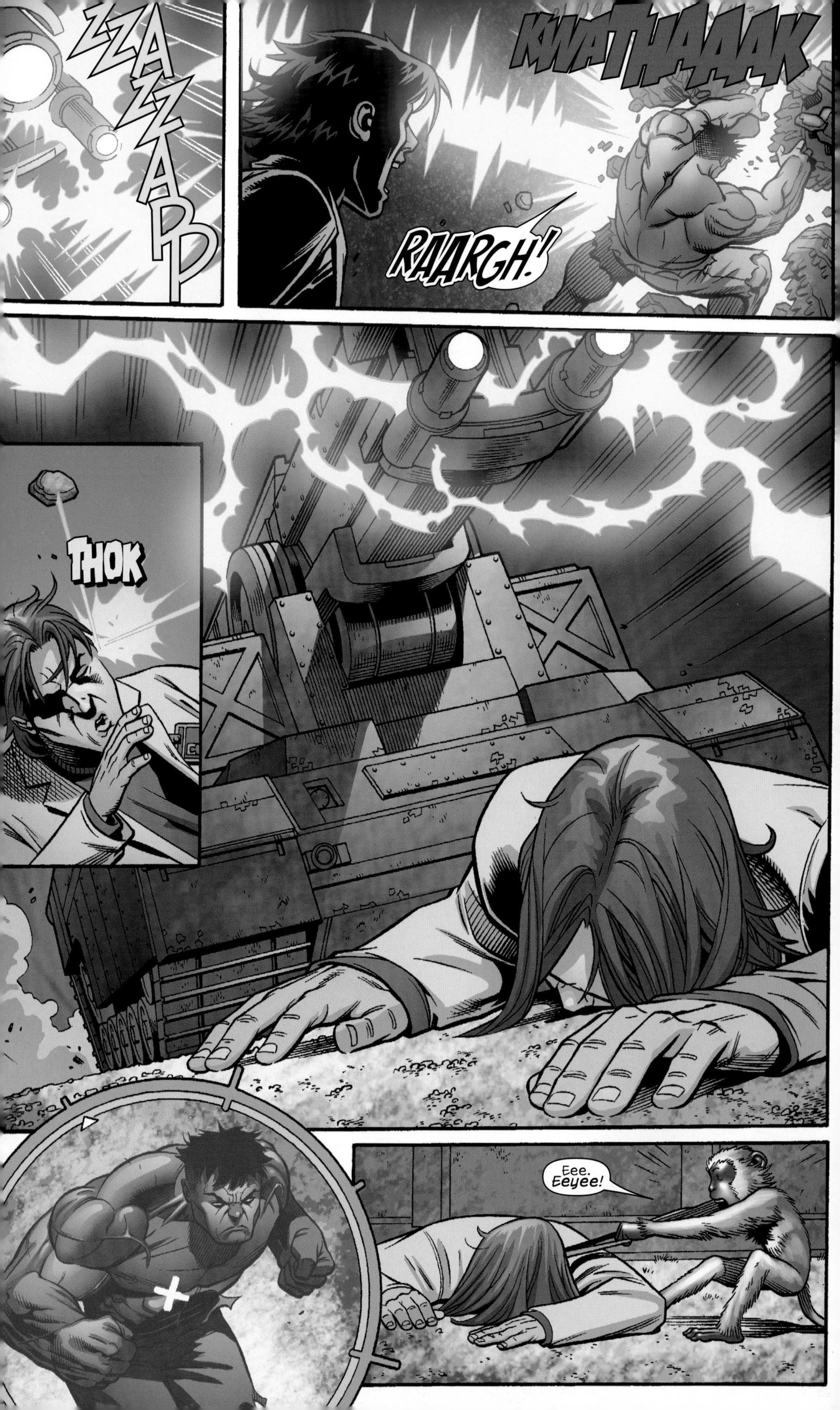

ZZAZZAP
KWATHAAAK
RAARGH!
THOK
Eee.
Eeyee!

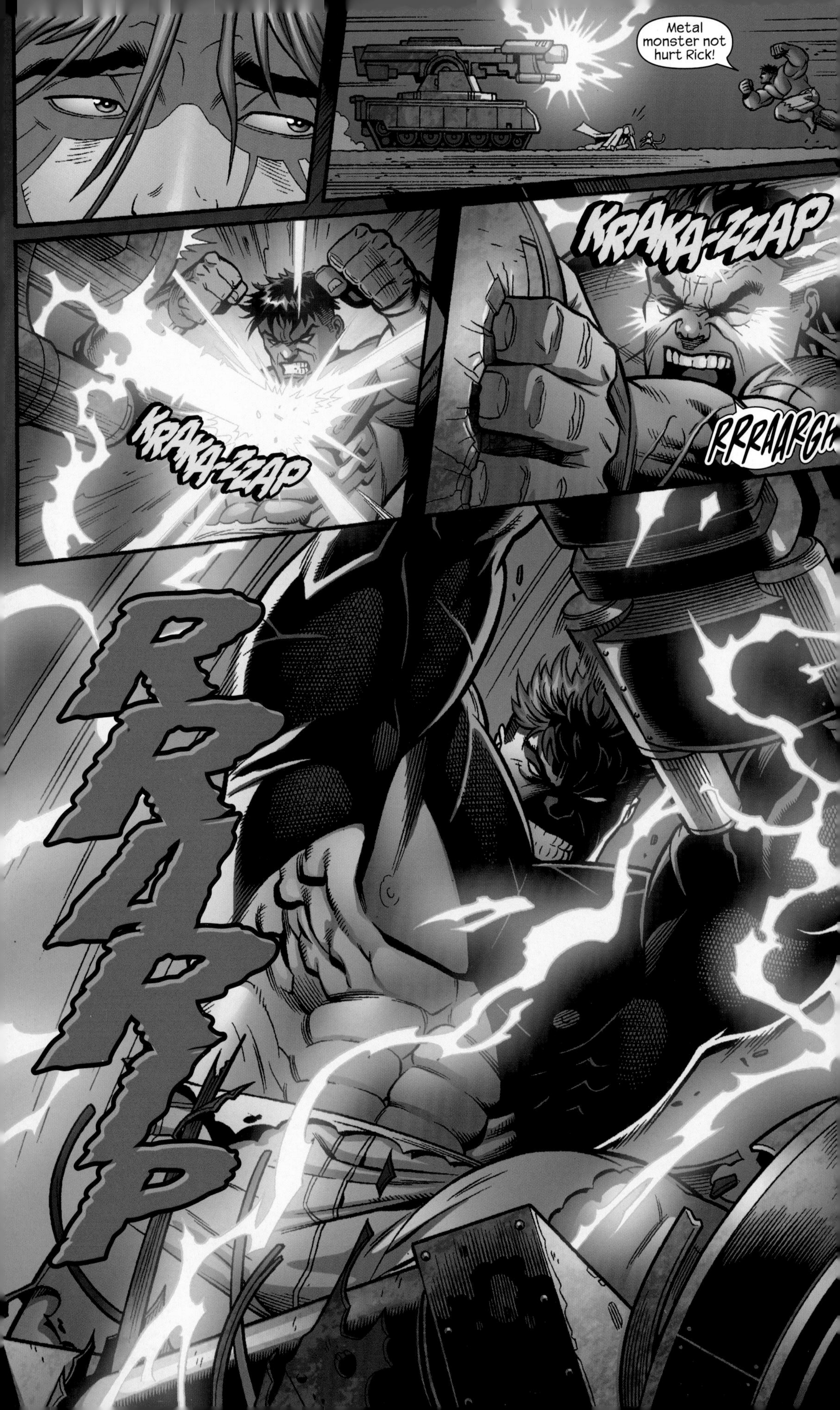

Metal monster not hurt Rick!
KRAKA-ZZAP
KRAKA-ZZAP
RRRAARGH
RRRAAGH

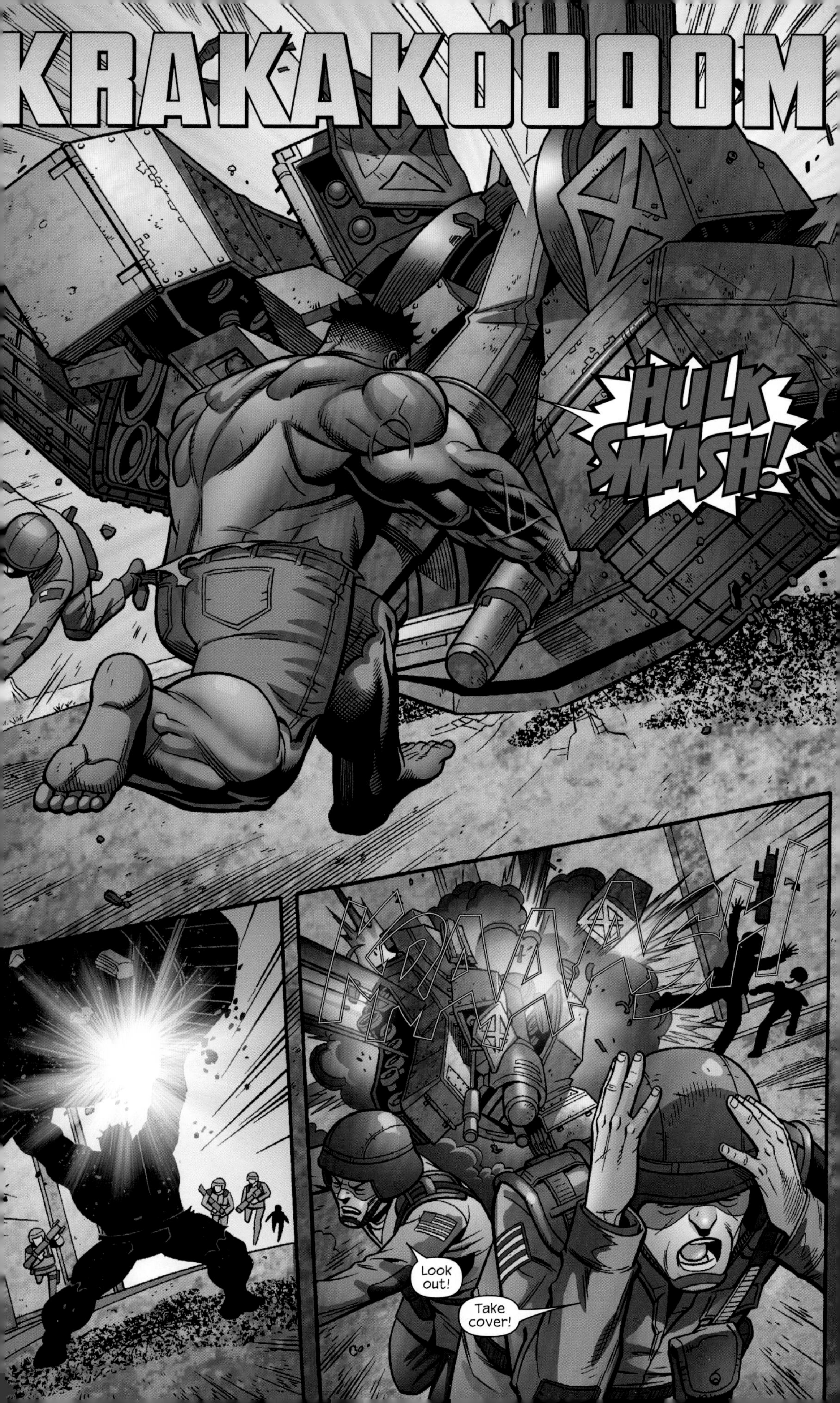
KRAKAKOOOOM
HULK SMASH!
Look out!
Take cover!

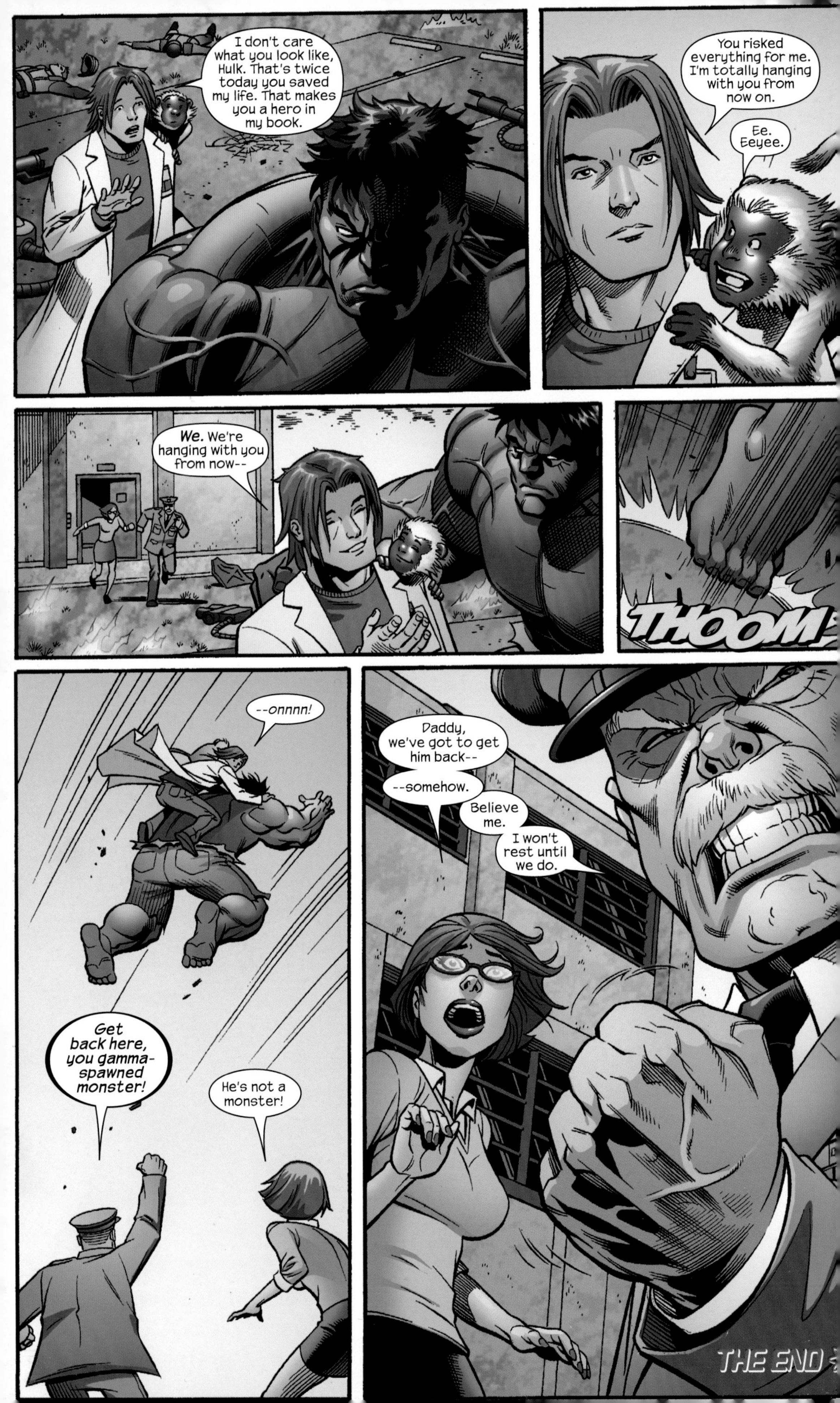
I don't care what you look like, Hulk. That's twice today you saved my life. That makes you a hero in my book.
You risked everything for me. I'm totally hanging with you from now on.
Ee. Eeyee.
We. We're hanging with you from now--
THOOM
--onnnn!
Get back here, you gamma-spawned monster!
He's not a monster!
Daddy, we've got to get him back--
--somehow.
Believe me.
I won't rest until we do.
THE END